Welcome To The World

We are so excited to meet you!

Love, Kevin & Arlene Lowe

On the day
you were born
everything
changed.

The World is very **big** with lots of wonderful places to visit.

This is the beginning of
your amazing journey.

Your world is filled with beautiful things ...

tiny things ...

HUGE THINGS . . .

plants and flowers,
animals, birds
and insects

and so much COLOUR.

Oceans and deserts,
mountains and forests ...

laughter, love, wonder and joy.

As you grow,
make sure you
find time to chase
butterflies ...

Dance in the summer rain....

and search for fairies.

May your wishes
be granted

and your skies
filled with
sunshine.

Remember that

things will change

and time will fly.

Trust in yourself and reach for the stars.

The world is an exciting place, full of fun, adventure

and lots
and lots of
people.

There is only one

you

and to your
family and friends
YOU ARE
THEIR
WORLD!

Welcome To The World first published by Forget Me Not Books, an imprint of **FROM YOU TO ME LTD**, February 2017.
FROM YOU TO ME, Waterhouse, Waterhouse Lane, Monkton Combe, Bath, BA2 7JA, UK

FORGET® me NOT BOOKS

For a full range of all our titles where journals & books can also be personalised, please visit

WWW.FORGETMENOTBOOKS.COM

Written and illustrated by Lucy Tapper & Steve Wilson fromlucy.com

5 7 9 11 13 15 14 12 10 8 6 4

Printed and bound in China. This paper is manufactured from pulp
sourced from forests that are legally and sustainably managed.

Also available:
You're The Biggest